THE
SILVER
PONY

THE SILVER PONY

a story in pictures by LYND WARD

Houghton Mifflin Company · Boston

Library of Congress Catalog Card Number 72-5402
HC ISBN 0-395-14753-0
PA ISBN 0-395-64377-5

Printed in the United States of America

VB 20 19 18 17 16

THE
SILVER
PONY

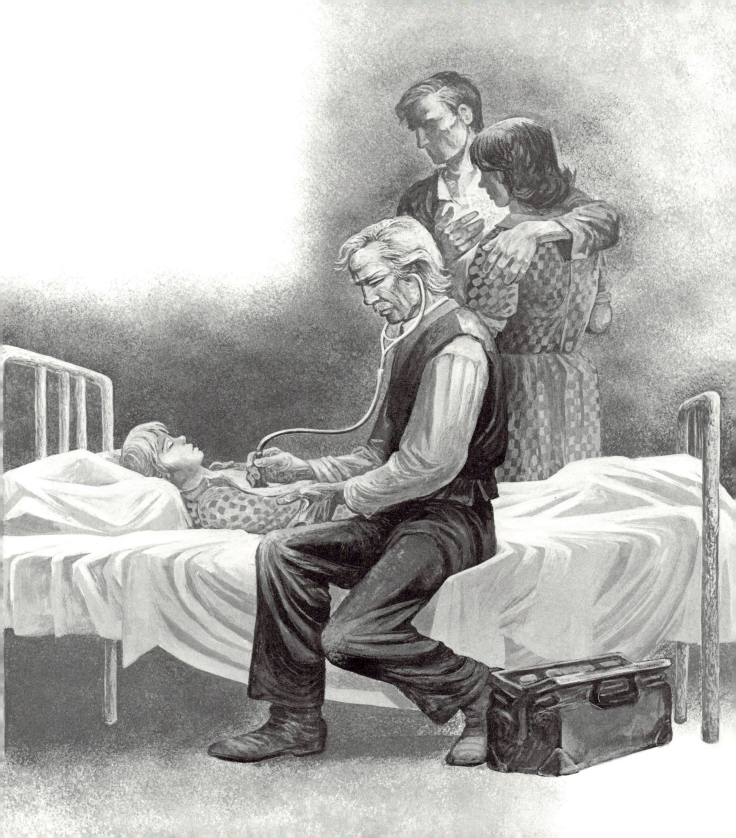